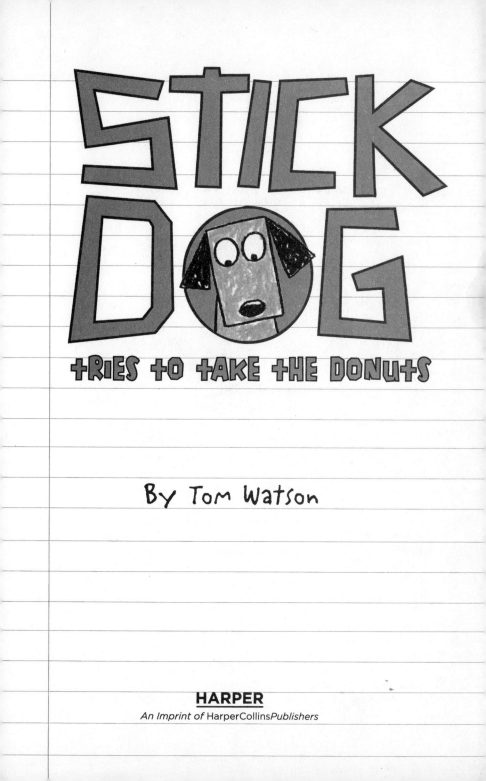

STICK DOG

tRiES tO tAKE tHE DONUtS

By Tom Watson

HARPER

An Imprint of HarperCollinsPublishers

Dedicated to Soo, Nancy, and Rob

Stick Dog Tries to Take the Donuts

Copyright © 2016 by Tom Watson

Illustrations by Ethan Long based on original sketches by Tom Watson

Library of Congress Control Number: 2015943576

ISBN 978-0-06-234320-8

ISBN 978-0-06-245715-8 (int.)

Typography by Jeff Shake

15 16 17 18 19   CG/RRDH   10 9 8 7 6 5 4 3 2 1

❖

First Edition

TABLE OF CONTENTS

Chapter 1

KAREN MAY LOSE HER MIND

It was early in the morning at Picasso Park, and Poo-Poo was doing what he does best.

He was running into something headfirst.

Thump b-brumm-m!

Thump b-brumm-m!

"One more time," Karen, the dachshund, said to Poo-Poo. "One more time should do it."

Poo-Poo, the poodle, lowered his head a third time and took aim at Karen's favorite garbage can. He built speed quickly over a few strides and struck the metal can right in the center.

Thump b-brum . . . Crash!

The garbage can fell onto its side, spilling its contents on the ground.

Quickly, Stick Dog, Stripes, and Mutt joined Karen to examine everything that had poured out. After rubbing his head against the cool, dew-covered grass, Poo-Poo joined them too.

"Thanks, Poo-Poo," Karen said as she sifted through the trash. "Nobody can hit things with their head like you."

"Well, I certainly love doing it," Poo-Poo said proudly, and bowed in acknowledgment.

"I've always wondered why you love hitting things with your head so much," Mutt said. He stepped carefully through the contents of the now-toppled garbage can. "It must be terribly painful."

"Oh, it is," replied Poo-Poo. "It hurts like the dickens. I've run into trees, cars,

and all kinds of other things on purpose.
Sometimes over and over again. And, man,
it's just an aching, searing pain every time
I do it."

Stripes, the Dalmatian, listened to all this
while she turned over some old newspaper
to see if there was any food underneath.
There wasn't. She asked, "Then why do you
do it, Poo-Poo?"

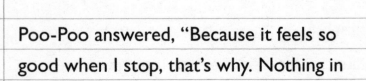

Poo-Poo answered, "Because it feels so
good when I stop, that's why. Nothing in

the world feels better than when you stop bashing your head into something over and over again. The thumping, throbbing pain slowly subsides. That feeling of not hurting myself is well worth it."

Stick Dog now looked at Poo-Poo. He had to confirm what he had just heard. "So, you hit your head on purpose because it feels so good to *stop* hitting your head on purpose?"

"Exactly."

"That makes sense," said Stripes.

"Sure does," Karen added.

Mutt, after tucking a broken pencil into his fur for safekeeping, agreed too. "I understand."

Stick Dog, frankly, didn't know what to say. So he decided not to say anything and changed the subject. "What do we have?" asked Stick Dog. "Anybody find anything?"

It had been a tough few days for the five dogs. They had only had creek water to drink and berries to eat. Their usual spots for food had been particularly unlucky lately. Nobody had grilled at the park in days. It was autumn, and the small humans were back in school. That meant there weren't any food vendors—hot dog carts, ice cream trucks, or churro wagons—

roaming around the neighborhood looking for hungry humans. It also meant fewer kids played in the park, leaving fewer tasty scraps in the garbage cans.

Stick Dog and his four friends had come to Karen's favorite garbage can almost as a last resort. She always had good luck here. And on many occasions, she had found her all-time favorite treat: barbecue potato chips.

Karen looked up at Stick Dog. "Nothing," she said dejectedly. "There's nothing here."

Stripes and Poo-Poo concurred.

But Mutt did not.

"What do you mean 'nothing'?" he asked. He was clearly surprised at Karen's answer and her disappointment. He quickly pawed out four items from the pile of garbage on the ground. "Look at all this stuff! Here's an old glove and a shoestring. A long, rusty nail—it's still sharp! And here's a crushed plastic water bottle!"

"She means there's nothing to eat, Mutt," Stick Dog explained.

"I beg to differ," Mutt said. He raised his eyebrows and picked up the glove with his mouth. He turned to Stick Dog and began to chew on the glove's thumb, and nodded his head.

"I mean nothing, umm, traditional to eat," Stick Dog explained further.

At this, Mutt dropped the glove and picked up the water bottle. Again, he began to chew and nod.

Stick Dog smiled. "Food, Mutt, food. We're looking for food. Not just stuff we can chew on."

Stripes, Karen, and Poo-Poo all turned to Stick Dog. Mutt tucked the plastic bottle, nail, shoestring, and old glove into his fur to save for later.

"I don't know, guys," Stick Dog said honestly. "I don't know what we're going to do. I guess we could go look for some more berries. We'll have to swim across the creek.

We've picked every last berry on this side."

"If I eat one more berry, I think I'm going to lose it," Karen said.

"Lose what?" asked Mutt. "Lose the berry?"

"It's an expression." Karen sighed. "It means, like, lose your mind."

"Huh?" asked Mutt. He was trying his best to understand. "How can you lose your mind? It's not like an old sock or a Frisbee. You don't put your mind somewhere and walk away and forget where you left it."

Now Stripes was interested too. "Yeah, Karen. If your brain is in a separate location, wouldn't it be thinking, 'Where's my body? I should go find it.'"

"Umm, I think what Karen's trying to say is—" offered Stick Dog, but he was interrupted by Poo-Poo.

"I've lost my mind a lot," he said matter-of-factly. "I can't remember how many times for some reason. But it's a big number, I think. When I bang headfirst into something extra-hard, I can't even think sometimes. I mean, I don't know where I am. I don't recognize anything around me. It's just blank.

Totally blank. So, I think you can lose your mind. I've done it."

"It's just an expression," Karen repeated. "I just don't want any more berries, that's all."

"Who said anything about berries?" Poo-Poo asked.

"Stick Dog did. Just now," answered Karen.

"Oh," Poo-Poo responded in a whisper. He looked suddenly puzzled. "Wait. What were we talking about?"

Stick Dog stepped in then. "I was talking about looking for berries to eat," he said. "Then Karen—"

But at that exact moment Stick Dog was

interrupted. He was not interrupted by one of his friends. A sound rang out from beyond Picasso Park.

Chapter 2

MR. DUMPTRUCK

They raced to the top of the tallest hill in Picasso Park to listen. They heard the sound again.

Bash-CLANG!!

"I don't know what that was," Poo-Poo answered, and tilted his head toward the southwest where the sound came from. "But it's coming from the northeast. Over by that old apple orchard."

"Erggh! I can't stand that place!" growled Stripes instantly. She had a cross look on

her face. Karen, Mutt, and Poo-Poo all bared
their teeth a little and began growling.

The old apple orchard was a torturous
place for them. There were only a couple
of dozen trees in it, and they had not been
tended to for a long, long time. Years ago,
a new blacktop road was built through the

middle of the orchard—and the owner had abandoned it. In late spring, the trees would burst to life with white and yellow blossoms. And in late summer and early autumn—right about this time of year—great red apples would grow to full ripeness.

They looked delicious.

They smelled delicious.

And the dogs could not get them.

Raccoons could get them. Birds could get them. Bees and other insects could get them. And, much to Poo-Poo's chagrin, squirrels could get them too.

But the dogs could not.

They avoided the area entirely at this time of year. To be so close to something so delicious—especially when they were often so, so hungry—was just too much to take.

"Let's stop thinking about food for a little while—and follow that strange sound," Stick Dog suggested in an attempt to change the subject. "If we obsess about our hunger too much, then it will just grow more severe. Sometimes I think it's better to put an idea aside for a while. You know, just ignore it. And then after we investigate that sound, maybe we'll have clearer minds—and we'll be able to think of a solution."

Stripes sighed—and then spoke.

"That's the nuttiest thing I've ever heard," she said, and shook her head slowly back and forth. "You mean we'll find food by trying *not* to find food? I mean, Stick Dog, that's a pretty crazy idea even for you."

"That's not quite what I—" Stick Dog began to explain, but he couldn't finish. Stripes continued her thought even louder.

"Old Stick Dog is off in one of his fan-ta-sy worlds again," she said. She wasn't just speaking loudly now. She was exaggerating or something. The words were sort of stretched out when she said them.

Sorry. I need to interrupt here. You remember that I'm allowed to take a break from the story sometimes, right? That's sort of our agreement.

Oh, and you're not allowed to complain about the pictures. I'm a pretty bad drawer, but you can't bug me about it. That's part of our agreement too.

Anyway, this thing that Stripes is doing with her voice is super-annoying, don't you think? You know who does it at my school?

My gym teacher, Mr. Pumpchuck.

That's his real name. I'm not kidding. We call him Mr. Dumptruck because he's big, slow, and intimidating.

Whenever it's my turn to do something—climb the rope to the ceiling, throw the dodgeball, shoot a free throw, whatever—he always makes a big announcement about it. It's how he ridicules my athletic skills. He thinks it's funny. He does it like this:

"Here comes T-O-M!" he yells. He stretches out all the words and syllables. "The f-aaa-bu-lous, ma-cho, to-tal ath-leeete T-O-M!"

So by stretching out his words like that,

Mr. Dumptruck's really telling my whole class that I'm not fabulous, macho, or totally athletic.

And here's the worst part: because he makes such a huge deal about it being my turn, it makes me extra-nervous and jittery because I know everybody is watching. And that makes me even less fabulous, macho, and athletic.

He did it yesterday in dodgeball.

You know what dodgeball is, right?

In case you don't, I'll sum it up for you.

Dodgeball is when a bunch of people run around a gym and throw things at each other as hard as they can. The more injuries the better.

Mr. Dumptruck loves dodgeball.

During yesterday's dodgeball game, he talked into the end of a baseball bat like it was a microphone and he was a sports commentator.

"Here comes a throw by the Suuu-per A-ma-zing T-O-M!" he announced.

Then I threw the ball and missed my target—Max Munson—by about thirty feet.

"Oh nooo-ooo!" Mr. Dumptruck announced. "Soo close, T-O-M!"

Nice, right?

Do you know who invented dodgeball? I do.

Cavemen.

I'm sure of it.

So, I know what Stick Dog is going through
as he's listening to Stripes. And, to be
honest, he deals with Stripes better than I
deal with Mr. Dumptruck. I could learn a lot
from Stick Dog actually.

Stripes continued, "Stick Dog's living in a ma-a-gi-cal place where food appears out of nowhere. It's a special place filled with ra-a-ain-bows and uni-corns and puf-f-fy clouds."

Stick Dog smiled and said, "No, that's not what—"

"I mean, really, Stick Dog," Stripes went on. "I'm surprised at you. We've worked together to find food for so long now. And it seems like Mutt, Karen, Poo-Poo, and I are always coming up with food-finding solutions. And now we need to do it again. You just go on living in that fan-ta-sy land—and we'll find something to eat. Right, guys?"

At this, Stripes looked around at the others.

They were not listening.

Poo-Poo had fallen asleep in the shade of a big willow tree. Karen was chasing her tail and not catching it. Mutt had managed to chew and swallow the pointer finger of that old glove and now worked on the pinkie.

Stripes didn't care that her friends were not paying attention.

"Stick Dog, don't you see? We have to be on a constant search for food," she continued in earnest. "We need total concentration all the time. We can't let one other thing enter our minds. That's the only way to survive. Complete and total focus!"

"I understand, Stripes. I really do," Stick Dog answered when he got the chance. "But maybe if we—"

"There is no MAYBE!" Stripes yelled. "TOTAL concentration! TOTAL focus! TOTAL commitment! TOTAL—"

BASH-Clang!

The metallic sound echoed in the air again.

"What was that?" Stripes screamed. Her head snapped back and forth to identify the location of the sound.

Poo-Poo woke up. Karen stopped chasing her tail. Mutt stood up and tucked the old glove back into his fur for later chewing satisfaction.

"We have to investigate!" Stripes said
urgently.

"But what about searching for—" Stick
Dog began to ask. But he couldn't finish his
question.

"Searching, smearching," Stripes said.
"Don't you want to go find out what that
is!?"

Stick Dog smiled. He answered, "Totally."

And off they went.

Chapter 3

POO-POO'S DENSITY

The dogs followed the clanging sound through the woods. Every minute or so they would stop, wait for the noise to ring out again, adjust their angle of pursuit, and move toward it.

Each time they stopped to listen, Poo-Poo took advantage of the opportunity to do his favorite thing: lift his head toward the higher branches and sniff for squirrels. "Those conniving, fuzzy puff-buckets are getting pretty smart," he said during one of these stops.

"You mean the squirrels, Poo-Poo?" asked Karen.

"That's right," Poo-Poo answered, and nodded curtly. "Those whisker-twitchers have become highly advanced, I think. The nut-dropping scoundrels are hiding better than ever."

Mutt asked, "How do you think they're doing that?"

Poo-Poo was quick to answer. "Well,

obviously they've had to create a whole
new array of weapons and tools to combat
my superior squirrel-hunting skills. That's
certainly why it's so hard for me to find
them lately. Those stinky fur balls created
new methods and devices in a last-ditch
attempt to cling to any final hope for species
survival. They had to do it to stand any
chance against me."

His friends were quite impressed with this
concept. Mutt asked, "What new tools have
they developed, Poo-Poo?"

"I wish I knew, Mutt. I wish I knew,"
answered Poo-Poo. "I wouldn't be surprised
if they now have cloaking devices to hide
themselves from my tremendous sniffing
abilities. Or perhaps they invented a
camouflage machine. I bet they scurry into it

whenever their radar devices detect I'm in the area."

"Camouflage machine?" Karen asked. "Radar devices?"

"For sure," Poo-Poo said, and nodded with absolute confidence. "It's why I can't find those nasty fluff balls. It's the only explanation I can think of."

Stripes, Mutt, and Karen were almost awestruck by everything Poo-Poo said. They followed each of his words with wide-open eyes and utter concentration. He had worked himself up into a pretty good frenzy.

"Each one of those sniffy whisker-flickers drives me nuts!" Poo-Poo sneered. He spoke through clenched teeth as he paced back and forth. "They're my archenemies! My daily obsession! My . . . my . . . my . . . whole reason for living. I was BORN to prove my superiority to squirrels! It's my life's work! It's my DENSITY!"

"I think you mean 'destiny,'" Stick Dog said quietly, but nobody heard him. They were too wrapped up in Poo-Poo's emotional tirade.

He continued to talk to himself as much as to the others. "If I could just get up into those trees, I'd find those poof-tails," he muttered, and paced some more. "One time. That's all I need. Just one time up in a tree. No cloaking device could hide them from me. No radar could detect me. No, sir. If I could get up in a tree and confront a squirrel face-to-face, it would be all over. All over, I tell you."

As Poo-Poo ranted, Stick Dog continued to wonder about the sound. He thought they were pretty close. And he hoped the investigation into that sound would take

Poo-Poo's mind off squirrels—and take everybody else's minds off their hunger. He knew his friends were hungry. Berries and creek water were not enough to subsist on. Stick Dog was running out of ideas. He was worried, but he didn't want his friends to know that.

Investigating that sound might distract his friends from their hunger. And it would buy Stick Dog some time, perhaps, to think of another food source. His first job, however, was to end Poo-Poo's latest squirrel obsession. He stepped closer to him.

"I'm sorry you can't get up in a tree, Poo-Poo," Stick Dog said seriously. "I'm sure— heck, I'm positive—that if you did, you would prove yourself against a squirrel."

"You bet I would."

"But for now, let's keep moving toward that—"

Smash-CLANG!!

The sound was close.

Really close.

Its loudness and proximity startled all five dogs.

"It's this way!" yelled Stripes.

"Let's go!!" screamed Poo-Poo.

And that's exactly what they did.

Chapter 4

PERCHING AND SWOOPING

Stick Dog and his four friends passed through a clump of about a dozen apple trees and emerged from the forest. Along the edge of the woods ran a long, straight blacktop road. Directly across the road there were several more apple trees.

Stick Dog immediately noticed two peculiar, unfamiliar things as he scanned their surroundings. The first was an odd building about a mile down the road. It had two large, spinning objects on its roof. One was a giant cup, which had the word "Dizzy's" on it. Stick Dog figured it was dizzy because it was spinning on the roof so much. The other huge, rotating object was even stranger. It was a hollow circle—like a giant truck tire and painted pink. It had the word "Donuts" on it. Stick Dog had never heard that word before.

The second weird thing Stick Dog noticed was much closer. Parked on the other side of the road by a tall telephone pole was a large, odd-looking truck. It had a long, jointed crane that stretched high in the air.

A human in a yellow hard hat was near the
top of the pole, standing on a small platform.
He worked on a metallic box with black
wires running in and out of it. The man had
thick, muscular arms. He wore overalls,
big brown work boots, and a faded-yellow
T-shirt.

The dogs stood
completely still behind
a big, fallen tree branch.
They were well hidden
among its brown leaves and
twigs. They had never seen
this kind of truck before.
And they had certainly never
seen a man at the top of a
telephone pole before.

"What in the world is that
man doing up there, Stick
Dog?" Poo-Poo asked in
wonder.

Before Stick Dog could answer, Karen provided an explanation. "He's perched," she began to explain. "I see birds up on poles and wires like that all the time. They wait for a small animal like a mouse to come out, then they swoop down and snatch it and eat it. That's what he's doing up there. He's waiting to see something scamper around on the ground to eat."

"That makes sense," Mutt said.

"I see," said Stripes.

Poo-Poo nodded along as well.

"So, umm—" Stick Dog said, and stopped. He tried to think of a polite way to say something. "You think he's going to jump down and—"

"Swoop down," Karen corrected.

"Right, swoop down," said Stick Dog. "You think he's going to swoop down from all the way up there to get a mouse to eat?"

"Oh, Stick Dog, Stick Dog," Karen said, and shook her head in a sad kind of way. "Humans don't eat mouses, Stick Dog."

"Mice," corrected Stick Dog.

"Yeah, that's what I said," Karen answered.

"They don't eat mice. He's waiting for human food to swoop down on."

"Human food?" asked Stick Dog.

"That's right." Karen seemed very sure of herself. "You know: hamburgers, frankfurters, pizza, ice cream—that kind of thing."

At the mention of all these foods, which the dogs had tasted before, their stomachs began to gurgle and grumble. They began to salivate and drool at the tasty memories.

Stick Dog watched the man high in the air. While he did, he asked, "Karen, when the birds are perched and the mice come out, where do they come out from?"

"Little holes in the ground, of course," Karen whispered. She was still drooling and remembering.

"And when humans are perched up there, where do the frankfurters, pizza, ice cream, and hamburgers come from?"

Karen stopped drooling. She wiped her lips. "Stick Dog," she said seriously. "I'm not a hamburger. Or a pizza. Or a frankfurter. Or an ice cream. I don't know where they come from."

Stick Dog asked, "And doesn't the human

need wings to swoop?"

"I don't know."

"Isn't he too heavy?"

"I'm not sure."

"How do humans get up to the top? Not everybody has a truck like this guy."

"No idea."

Karen then looked at Mutt, Poo-Poo, and Stripes and sort of raised her left eyebrow in Stick Dog's direction a couple of times. Her mouth was pulled up on one side, and her eyes darted back and forth between Stick Dog and the others.

"Stick Dog," she said with that smirk on her face. "You really seem to be a little too caught up in the details of this whole thing."

Stick Dog might have continued to quiz Karen, but their stomach grumblings were too loud to ignore.

Mutt said what everybody was now thinking. "All this talk about hamburgers and pizza and stuff has made me more hungry. And those darn apples up there are taunting me! We have got to go find some food!"

"But shouldn't we wait here for the human food to emerge?" asked Stick Dog. He smiled a bit to himself. "Then we can race in and try to get it before the human swoops down."

"We're hungry NOW, Stick Dog!" Poo-Poo exclaimed. "We can't wait for that!"

Stick Dog smiled again. "Okay," he said. "Let's go."

And they probably would have left right then.

But they didn't.

Do you know why?

I'll tell you.

It's because right then the man stepped off the platform and into a basket at the end of the truck's mechanical arm. He began to descend from high in the air.

"What's happening?!" yelped Stripes.

"He's swooping!" Karen said immediately.

Chapter 5

THE SCENT OF STRAWBERRIES

Stick Dog watched as the big man used his hands on a joystick inside the narrow basket at the end of the crane. A motor whirred to life. Stick Dog couldn't be sure, but it looked like the man controlled the speed and direction of his descent with the joystick.

When Karen saw the man come down, she instantly began to scan the ground for pizza, frankfurters, and other human food.

She didn't see any—much to her own surprise.

Stick Dog saw the disappointment on her face. "He's probably coming down for something else," he said to Karen. "Maybe he'll swoop for food later."

This made Karen feel better.

The huge mechanical arm reached the ground, and the man stepped out of the basket. He came to the back of the truck where the dogs could easily see him.

The man opened a large, metal toolbox, tossed in a heavy screwdriver, and let the lid slam shut. It sounded like this: *Bash-Clang!*

"That's the sound we heard," Stripes said.

Stick Dog nodded.

"Now that we've identified the sound, Stick Dog, can we *please* go on a food search?" asked Mutt.

"Yeah, Stick Dog!" Karen chimed in. So did Poo-Poo and Stripes.

Stick Dog listened to his friends' request while he watched the man at the back of his truck. Now that he had put some tools away, the man did something else.

"Stick Dog?" asked Mutt.

"Just a minute, please," Stick Dog replied.
He was disappointed that their investigation
had not turned into a longer adventure—a
better distraction—for his friends. He had
wanted to take their minds off food—well,
their lack of food—for a while. Instead,
Karen's misguided and ridiculous theory
that the man would swoop down from the
telephone pole and snatch nonexistent
hamburgers, pizza, frankfurters, and ice
cream from the ground had actually done
the opposite thing: they were thinking
about food even more than before. They
were hungrier than ever.

"Can we go now?" Karen asked.

"Shh." He knew they were starving. But there was a reason why he wanted to observe this man at the back of his truck a little longer. Stick Dog's instincts were kicking in.

"Are you even listening to us?" Stripes asked.

"Shh," Stick Dog requested again politely. Then the man reached his hand into a box and pulled out a light-brown ball. It didn't appear to be a tool. It was round and sort of flat. It fit perfectly into his hand. The man didn't bounce it or toss it up in the air as Stick Dog suspected he would. He did something totally surprising.

The man took that ball and brought it to his mouth.

And he took a bite out of it.

Stick Dog couldn't believe his eyes. He stared at the man as he chewed and swallowed that first bite. He had a very happy and satisfied look on his face. His mouth was turned up in a small grin, his eyelids drooped a little, and he nodded his head.

The man at the truck took a second bite. When he did, Stick Dog saw that the ball had a red liquid center. It was very peculiar, and Stick Dog took a sniff of the air in the man's direction. Oddly, Stick Dog picked up the scent of strawberries even though he knew they were out of season. They'd picked their last wild strawberry more than a month ago.

Some of that red juice—it actually looked thicker than juice—was on the man's lower lip. Stick Dog watched as he used his index finger to wipe it off. Then the man licked his finger, smiled, and finished eating the thing.

Stick Dog stopped watching when Poo-Poo spoke.

"Let's go already!" Poo-Poo insisted. "We need to find food!"

Stick Dog turned to his friends and smiled. He looked at each of them one at a time, meeting their eyes with a determined gaze. All he said was, "We already have."

Poo-Poo asked, "Where?"

"There," Stick Dog said, and pointed toward the man.

The man took a jacket that hung from a corner of the truck and tossed it into the back. The sun was bright and warm and Stick Dog figured the man wouldn't need it. As it fell, the jacket captured some air under it like a parachute and fluttered down softly to its landing. Then the man stretched his arms over his head and gave his shoulders a quick shake.

"He's not eating, Stick Dog. There's no food," Poo-Poo said. "I think he's dancing. He's not a very good dancer. I mean, that guy's got no moves at all."

"He's waking up," Stick Dog answered, and watched some more. "And you're right. He's not eating just this second. But watch."

As if on Stick Dog's cue, the man reached into the box and took out a second object. This one was totally different from the first. It didn't have a red liquid center. In fact, it didn't have a center at all. Stick Dog was very curious about it. It was covered in pink paint or goo or something. It had small colored specks all over it too. It looked, Stick Dog now realized, like a much smaller version of the huge truck tire thing that spun around on the roof of that building down the road.

The worker opened his mouth and took a huge bite of it, licking some of the pink stuff from his lips.

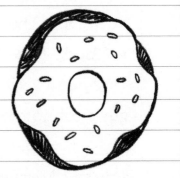

"That's definitely food!" whispered Stick Dog.

Chapter 6

THE DONUT DISCOVERY

"You don't know that it's food for sure," Poo-Poo said.

"Yeah, Stick Dog," Stripes added immediately after. "It might not be."

"It could be anything else," Mutt concurred.

Karen was too busy to join in the conversation. She had discovered an itch when she rubbed her belly on the ground, and it now demanded her full attention. It appeared to be super-difficult for her to get at the itch. As you know, she has really short legs, and this makes reaching things—even itches—frustrating for her.

"Of course it's food," Stick Dog said. "He's taking bites of those things—whatever they are. And then he's chewing. See his mouth shift around? See his jaw move up and down? And look: you can even see his neck bump in and out when he swallows. He's eating. He's eating food."

"I think that first thing was a deflated ball, Stick Dog. The second thing is a small pink Frisbee. Not food," Poo-Poo said, sounding doubtful. "Balls and Frisbees aren't for eating. They're for fetching."

"I thought that first one was a ball too," said Stick Dog. "But when—"

"Excuse me, Poo-Poo," Mutt said before Stick Dog could finish. He rarely interrupted anyone, but this time he seemed to have a rather important point to make. "But I've eaten several balls and Frisbees myself. I'm kind of an expert on the subject."

Stripes didn't seem very convinced. "I don't think that means they're food, Mutt."

"I don't think those things are balls or Frisbees anyway," Stick Dog interjected. "And that's not really the issue here. We may have found a new food source. It's certainly worth trying to figure out."

But nobody paid him any attention. Stripes, Mutt, and Poo-Poo had become instantly obsessed with whether rubbery things like balls and Frisbees could be defined as food. And Karen had not satisfied her itch yet. She had moved a few feet to her left to find a rougher patch of ground with twigs and dry leaves. She hoped this new area would offer greater scratching capability.

"I know you eat plastic things and rubber things, Mutt," Poo-Poo said. "I just don't know if they qualify as food."

"Some of them can be quite satisfying, let me tell you," Mutt said quickly. "I've consumed a couple of Frisbees, for instance. I just start chewing on the edges, you know? I love chewing. It passes the time so wonderfully. It's got a nice rhythm to it.

You know what I mean?"

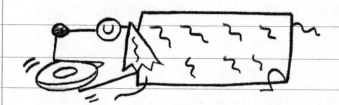

"Umm, sort of," Stripes said. She'd never eaten any plastic or rubber objects herself. It didn't seem like a very appetizing idea to her, but she didn't want to be rude. "I guess."

"Well, chewing just has such a soothing tempo to it," Mutt continued to explain. "I sort of go into a trance. My eyelids get real heavy and sleepy. And then before I even know how much time has gone by, I look down, and there's no more Frisbee or ball or whatever left. It's disappeared! Because I ate it! That's why I think balls and Frisbees can truly be called food."

Stripes nodded. She seemed to have come around to Mutt's way of thinking.

Stick Dog, meanwhile, continued to observe the big worker in the hard hat. The man had just finished eating the pink circle and closed the lid to the box. Most important, Stick Dog suspected there might be more of those edible objects in the box. And the box itself sat on the back bumper of the truck.

The man then lifted an enormous Styrofoam cup and removed its lid. The cup said "Dizzy's Big GULP Coffee" on it. When he took the lid off, a cloud of steam escaped from inside the cup. The worker blew into the cup and took a long, slow sip.

His face showed great satisfaction after this—as if that drink was something he had waited for all morning. His lips tightened. He smiled a bit and nodded his head at the cup like he was saying thank you to it or something.

Stick Dog watched him carefully.

Karen scratched her belly.

But Poo-Poo, after considering Mutt's argument, still was not convinced that rubber things were food. "I don't think you can call something like a Frisbee food. Food has to have flavor. I think that's really important."

"Hey," Mutt said. He seemed slightly taken aback. "I've had a couple of delicious Frisbees, Poo-Poo. It's an acquired taste, I'll grant you that. But they *do* have flavor."

Poo-Poo said, "I just don't think it's food. It's not *food* food. It's just something you eat."

Upon hearing this, Mutt defended his
position. "No, no. If you eat it, it's food. The
eating part is the deciding factor."

This made Stripes rejoin the conversation.
"So when it's a ball at Picasso Park, then
it's just a ball. But when you retrieve the
ball and begin chewing on it, that's when it
becomes food? Is that what you're saying?"

Mutt shook his head. "Not quite," he
explained. "I think during the delightful
biting-and-chewing experience, it's still a ball.
Only when actual swallowing takes place
does it become food."

"So when the chewed-up piece of ball
moves from your mouth to your stomach, it
mutates into food?" asked Stripes.

"Something like that," Mutt answered. He seemed to appreciate that Stripes was trying to understand. "I think it's more like a transformation. It's a little more magical—a little more mystical."

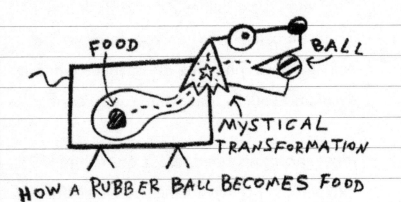

FOOD

BALL

MYSTICAL TRANSFORMATION

HOW A RUBBER BALL BECOMES FOOD

Stripes seemed to buy into this concept. She nodded along as Mutt spoke.

Karen now stood up. She had scratched her belly itch away successfully. The dry twigs on the ground had helped.

Stick Dog watched as the man put the huge cup down. He reached into his toolbox again. He removed a large pair of pliers and an abnormally big pair of scissors.

"Okay, then," Poo-Poo said. He wanted to make one last point. There was an air of confidence about him. He looked suddenly satisfied at coming up with a foolproof argument. "What about when you're chewing *and* swallowing at the same time? Sometimes you're swallowing one bunch of food while there's still another bunch in your mouth. It can't be a ball and food at the same time! That's impossible. I think I've proven my point. So there!"

Mutt seemed surprised at this turn of the conversation. It was a good point—and he knew it. He was puzzled by it—but only for a few seconds. Then he simply said, "That's the mystical part."

This would have likely gone on for some time, but just then a sudden loud noise rang out.

CLANG!

The man had tossed a ball-peen hammer into his box.

This grabbed all of their attention at once—well, all of their attention except Stick Dog's. He was already watching while the others debated the definition of "food" and Karen scratched her belly.

The man picked up his toolbox and climbed into the narrow compartment at the end of the long, mechanical crane. Using his fingers to manipulate the joystick and control the crane, he rose high in the air. When he got to the top of the telephone pole, the man stepped out of the basket and onto the platform.

Stick Dog couldn't believe it.

They had been here for only a short while and had found food. More miraculously, the human eating the food had just left—and left the food behind. Stick Dog could see the box sitting on the back of the truck right next to the big Styrofoam cup.

Stick Dog stared up at the man at the top of the pole. His back was turned as he worked.

He looked pretty busy. Stick Dog thought there was a pretty good chance the man would remain turned that way. And even if he did look around and discover them, by the time he came down with that long crane, the dogs would have plenty of time to escape into the forest.

"Come on!" Stick Dog whispered urgently. "Now's our chance!"

"Chance to what?" Poo-Poo asked.

"Our chance to get some of those things the human was eating!"

"Oh, that," said Poo-Poo. "Don't you think we should first decide if they're food or not? We've had quite a spirited discussion about the subject while you dillydallyed about with whatever you were doing. Shouldn't we settle the debate first?"

"We can talk more about it later if you'd like," Stick Dog said kindly. "Right now, let's just go have a look. It looked like that human thought those things were really tasty."

This was enough to get Poo-Poo and the others moving. They followed Stick Dog out from the edge of the woods—and carefully across the street to the truck. In just fourteen seconds, Stick Dog was up on his hind legs. He could reach the box easily. He folded the box flaps back. He read "Dizzy's

Donuts—A Baker's Dozen in Every Box!"
as he flipped the flaps open.

There were eleven more circular objects
in the box. There were a couple of pink
ones with speckles, some covered in white
powder, and some light brown and dark
brown circles as well. Some of them were
shiny and some were not.

"There are a lot in here, but we'll just take
one for now. I don't think he'll notice if only
one is missing," Stick Dog whispered. He
plucked a pink one out and held it carefully
in his mouth.

Stick Dog pushed the box flaps closed with his nose and noticed a sticker that read, "2 for 1 special! Buy one box, get another free!" There was no time to think about what that meant. He wanted to get back to safety as fast as possible.

Stick Dog nodded toward the woods and ran that way. Mutt, Stripes, Poo-Poo, and Karen followed close behind.

Once they were well hidden among the apple trees and brush again, Stick Dog used his paws to tear the pink speckled circle into five roughly equal parts. He was careful to take the smallest portion for himself.

Poo-Poo finished his bite first and instantly declared, "That was no rubber ball! Or Frisbee." He lifted his head in the air, closed his eyes, and moved his tongue around inside his mouth to both recapture and remember the flavors. Then he added, "It combines a sudden sugar rush with a light, airy texture. For being such a small thing, it's packed with sweetness and power."

"Just like me," Karen said, and giggled.

Poo-Poo, who didn't appreciate having his food descriptions interrupted, gave Karen a quick and curt glance, but she was already stepping away from the others for some reason. Maybe she had another itch.

"Like I was saying," Poo-Poo continued. "This combination of sweetness and texture manages to both awaken my palate and satisfy—in a small way—my stomach. I don't know what those things are, but I LOVE them!"

The other dogs all agreed. Well, Karen didn't agree. She wasn't there anymore.

"They're called 'donuts,'" Stick Dog said. He too savored the lingering flavor in his mouth. "It said so on the box."

"'Donuts,' huh?" Poo-Poo said. He seemed to be testing out this word he had never heard before. "Well, I'm a big fan of these so-called 'donuts.'"

"Me too!" said Mutt and Stripes simultaneously.

"Well, there are plenty more in the box. We just need to wait for the right time to go back and get them," encouraged Stick Dog. Mutt, Stripes, and Poo-Poo gathered around him then. Their faces were eager and enthusiastic. They wanted more donuts, that was certain.

But something was wrong.

Someone was missing.

And it only took Stick Dog one-third of one second to notice. Quickly, he asked the others, "Where did Karen go?"

It didn't take long to find her.

Stick Dog snapped his head around to look at the truck.

Karen was there. She had pulled herself up to the back bumper and was standing on it.

Stick Dog looked down at the ground, closed his eyes, and shook his head slowly back and forth. When he lifted his head to take another look, he could see Karen's body—but not her head.

And he could see something else too.

The worker up on the platform was looking for something on his tool belt. He couldn't seem to find whatever he needed. He climbed back into the basket and put his fingers on the joystick. He was coming down.

And headed right toward Karen.

Chapter 7

BIG GULP COFFEE

Stick Dog heard the truck's mechanical arm whir to life. The worker concentrated on the joystick device that controlled the truck's arm. Stick Dog didn't think the man could see Karen from the angle of his descent. Stick Dog estimated he had a little more than one minute to get Karen back before the man reached the ground. That wasn't much time.

"Karen!" he called quietly. Stick Dog was concealed safely behind some old, fallen branches, but he couldn't risk calling too loudly. "Karen! Get back here!"

"Where is she, Stick Dog?" Mutt asked. He, Poo-Poo, and Stripes now peered through the tree branches and foliage too.

"She's right there," Stick Dog said, and pointed with his nose. "She's got her head in that big Styrofoam cup."

"How do you know that's her?" asked Poo-Poo in a whisper.

Stick Dog hesitated for a split second before answering. "It's her tail and her body sticking out of the cup. Don't you see?"

Poo-Poo answered, "I see all that, yes. But

it's really the head that makes a dog, don't you think? And we can't see that thing's head. It might not be Karen at all."

Stick Dog couldn't believe what he heard.

"Yes, Stick Dog. It could be anybody," Stripes chimed in.

The man was fifty-seven seconds away.

"Maybe it's Phyllis, the raccoon," Mutt suggested. He always tried to help in this kind of way.

Stick Dog decided instantly not to partake in any further discussion with Poo-Poo, Mutt, and

Stripes. Instead he called out sharply again, "Karen! Karen! The big man's coming back!"

Karen's body didn't move in any way to indicate she heard Stick Dog. In fact, it seemed that she pushed her head even farther into the cup.

The man was forty-six seconds away.

Meanwhile, the conversation among Mutt, Stripes, and Poo-Poo continued.

"I don't think it's Phyllis, Mutt," said Poo-Poo. "Raccoons have striped, puffy tails. And that tail sticking out of the cup isn't puffy at all. That tail is more like a giraffe's, I think. Maybe there's a giraffe in the cup."

"Good point," Mutt
conceded.

"Karen!!" Stick Dog
called again.

The man was thirty-
seven seconds away.

"Maybe it's a raccoon
who had its tail
groomed," suggested Stripes.

"Hey, you know what?" Poo-Poo said
suddenly. It seemed as if a new idea had
popped into his mind. "You know whose tail
that *does* look like?"

"Whose?" Mutt and Stripes asked in unison.

The man was twenty-eight seconds away from descending all the way down to the ground—and climbing out of the basket. And Karen couldn't even see him coming.

Stick Dog understood the problem. Karen had burrowed her head so deep into that large Styrofoam cup that her ears were inside. She couldn't hear him.

In the meantime, Poo-Poo answered Stripes and Mutt. He exclaimed, "That tail looks like Karen's! I wonder if that might be her."

"Hmm, I never thought of that," said Mutt.

"It's possible, I guess," said Stripes. She didn't sound completely convinced yet.

The man was nineteen seconds away.

"Hey, Stick Dog!" Poo-Poo said, and twisted around to face him. "I think it might be Karen in that cup. Hey, where's Stick Dog?"

But Stick Dog didn't hear Poo-Poo at all. He had already leaped from the forest's edge and raced toward Karen. When he reached the truck, he placed his front paws on the back bumper. He bit down softly on the loose skin at the back of Karen's neck—she hadn't, thank goodness, pushed any farther into the cup.

"I found him," Poo-Poo said slowly as he stared out of the woods. He couldn't quite comprehend what was happening. He couldn't understand why Stick Dog had Karen in his mouth.

Neither could the others apparently.

"Why is he eating Karen?" Mutt asked. "I mean, if it's even her."

"He's been hungry before," Stripes added. "But never so hungry that he ate one of us. At least, as far as I can remember. I'm almost certain he's never eaten me."

"Although, I must say, Karen does look rather delicious, if you think about it," said Poo-Poo as he watched Stick Dog struggle to return as quickly as he could with Karen in his mouth. The truck's arm was almost all the way down now. And its whirring motor slowed and made less noise. "Remember that time she imitated a frankfurter? I have to admit, she was a pretty good-looking frankfurter."

"True," Mutt said.

By this time, of course, Stick Dog was nearly back to them. When he made it into the woods with the others, he set Karen down on the ground and slowly unclenched his grip on the nape of her neck.

Because the large cup was still on her head, they couldn't really tell if she even noticed being set down at all. In fact, the only motion she made was to push her head farther into the cup again.

The big man was out of the basket and standing at the back of the truck now. The motor was completely shut down. Stick Dog had made it back into the forest cover just in time.

He stood there panting to catch his breath. Karen was small—all dachshunds are—but Stick Dog was surprised at just how heavy she actually was. It had not been easy to sprint back to safety with her in his mouth. As he tried to catch his breath, Karen shoved her head deeper into the cup. Mutt, Poo-Poo, and Stripes stepped closer to him.

"Stick Dog," Mutt said.

Stick Dog nodded toward him. He was panting too hard to answer. But he smiled at Mutt, Stripes, and Poo-Poo as they approached. He knew they were about to congratulate him. Rescuing Karen had not been easy, after all.

"We have something to say to you," Mutt began. He seemed to be speaking for the other two.

Stick Dog nodded again.

"I don't know how to say this," Mutt
continued, then paused in a sort of
awkward and uncomfortable way. He
inhaled deeply and said, "Poo-Poo, Stripes,
and I really don't think you should eat
Karen."

Stick Dog stared at
Mutt.

Now that Mutt
had broached the
subject, Poo-Poo and
Stripes joined in.

"It's really not very polite, Stick Dog,"
Stripes said. "I mean, I know you're hungry
and everything. We all are. But chewing on

Karen like that just doesn't seem right."

Stick Dog started to get his breath back a bit.

Poo-Poo asked, "You know that she isn't a frankfurter, right? She's not. She's a dog. A dog, Stick Dog. Not a frankfurter."

"I wasn't," Stick Dog panted, "eating her. I was rescuing her. That big guy came down from the top of the pole. And she couldn't hear him or see him because her head is stuffed inside that cup."

"Why did you stuff her head into the cup, Stick Dog?" Mutt asked sincerely. "Were you trying to hide her in there or what?"

"I didn't stuff her . . . ," Stick Dog began, but he was interrupted by Poo-Poo.

"I bet I know why," he said. His face had turned suddenly stern. His jaw was clenched tight, and he squinted his eyes slightly. "You tried to drink her first, didn't you, Stick Dog? You stuffed poor, little, helpless Karen into that cup to drink her. And when that didn't work out, you decided to eat her instead."

"That's terrible!" exclaimed Stripes.

Mutt shook his head sadly. "You should know better, Stick Dog."

By now, Stick Dog had caught his breath fully. And while you may think he would be mad that his friends had accused him of trying to eat (or drink) Karen, the opposite was actually true. He found it all sort of amusing. And now that Karen was safely back with them, he felt relief more than anything.

"You guys," said Stick Dog. "I wasn't trying to eat—or drink—Karen. She was about to be seen by that huge human. She couldn't hear me because her head is in the cup. I had to pick her up and bring her back."

"You were chewing on her, Stick Dog," said Poo-Poo. "We all saw it."

"That was the only way I could pick her up without hurting her. Look, I'll show you."

Stick Dog reached down and gently pulled the Styrofoam cup off Karen's head. It was stubbornly stuck for a few seconds, but then popped off easily.

"See, no bite marks or anything," Stick Dog said, and pointed. "I was very gentle."

Mutt, Stripes, and Poo-Poo examined Karen's neck while she licked furiously at the rim of the cup. There were a few brown drops of liquid there.

After a few seconds, Poo-Poo, Stripes, and Mutt apologized to Stick Dog. It turned out, they now realized, that he wasn't trying to eat (or drink) Karen after all. With that determined, their attention shifted quickly to her.

She was acting strangely.

"What do you want, Stick Dog?" Karen asked as she continued to lap at the rim of the cup. She didn't lift her head at all to speak, and her words came out faster than usual. "I heard you calling."

"You did?" Stick Dog was obviously surprised.

"Sure thing! Totally."

"Why didn't you answer?"

"I couldn't. I just couldn't! I *had* to finish drinking this brown liquid! Had to!" Karen exclaimed. She then gripped the cup's rim in her mouth. She tilted her head back in an attempt to get the very last drops from the bottom. When she finally shook the last drop out onto her tongue, Karen dropped the cup to the ground.

"You're talking funny," Stick Dog said to Karen. Then he looked at the cup that had now rolled to a stop. He read the words on the side out loud, "Dizzy's Big GULP Coffee."

"Coffee? That's what it's called?" Karen asked urgently. "I'm going to remember that. Coffee, coffee, coffee!"

COFFEE!?!

Stick Dog asked, "How full was that cup when you took your first drink?"

"Almost totally full. Almost totally. Real high. To the top. Not anymore though! It's empty. I drank every drop. I couldn't stop!" Karen said, and giggled.

"I see," said Stick Dog slowly.

"I see. You see. We all see. For coffee," Karen sang, and giggled again. "I just made that up. It rhymes and everything. Just made it up. Right here. Right now!"

"You seem kind of hyper or something," Stick Dog said.

While Stick Dog was extremely curious about Karen's hyperactivity and the strange new way she talked, the other dogs had lost interest. Their thoughts returned to far more urgent matters.

"We really do need to get some more of those donuts, Stick Dog," Poo-Poo said. He licked a few crumbs from his lips and whiskers. "That thing was fantastic!"

"Stick Dog?"

"Yes, Karen?"

"I'm going to chase my tail now," she said. "I just really need to move. Like right now. Fast."

"Umm, okay. Go ahead," Stick Dog said.

Karen immediately began chasing her tail with tremendous energy and glee. She spun clockwise for about half a minute. Then she stopped and panted for a few seconds. Instantly, she began chasing her tail counterclockwise just as fast. This process continued while Stick Dog and the others talked.

"I agree with Poo-Poo," Mutt said. "We should fetch some more of those donuts. Those things are scrumptious."

Stick Dog nodded and repeated, "I like the idea. But it will be tough getting past this guy."

He stopped to peer out at the man, hoping that maybe he had climbed into the basket to go to the top of the pole again.

He hadn't—but he was doing a most unusual thing. He searched all around on the ground and in the back of his truck and muttered to himself, "Coffee . . . coffee. Where did I put my coffee?"

At hearing this, Karen abruptly stopped spinning.

"Did someone say 'coffee'?!" she asked. "Let's get some. I'm in. Let's do it! Like right now."

"You really liked that coffee, didn't you, Karen?" asked Stripes.

"Liked it? I LOVED it! Coffee, coffee, coffee!!" Karen squealed. "Stick Dog?"

"Yes?"

"I'm going to run into the woods and back again, okay?"

"Umm," Stick Dog began to respond. But he didn't say anything else. Karen was already gone.

Stick Dog would have watched Karen—her behavior really was quite peculiar—but Stripes grabbed his attention.

She said, "Stick Dog, the man's leaving."

He was indeed. The man had picked up a wrench and climbed back into the mechanical arm's basket. Stick Dog heard him mutter to himself some more.

"Gotta find my coffee," he said before starting his ascent. "Must have left it up on the platform."

Stick Dog knew the man would be back up in the air in a minute—and their path would be clear. It was like a miracle. They had discovered this delicious new food source and the human was leaving it—again.

As soon as the man reached the top of the pole, they could sneak across the road and grab some more donuts. He knew there were plenty more in the box—he had seen them himself.

"Okay," Stick Dog said to Mutt, Poo-Poo, and Stripes. "As soon as Karen gets back, we'll go."

"I'm back!" Karen announced, and bumped into Mutt as she skidded and slid to a stop.

Stick Dog jumped back a little bit. He had not expected Karen to return so soon. But they were on a mission now—and their first task was to snatch some more donuts from the box. He would investigate Karen's spazziness later.

"The coast is clear," Stick Dog announced after looking in both directions down the road. The man was at the top of the pole and no vehicles were in sight. "Let's go!"

He scampered out of the woods, and the others scrambled behind him. It took just fourteen seconds for Stick Dog to cross the street and reach the truck. He crouched down by its side. He was pretty certain the man on the pole could not see him there. He checked behind to make certain the others were with him.

They were.

Except for Karen.

Chapter 8

WHERE IS KAREN THIS TIME?

"Where's Karen?!" Stick Dog asked. But before Poo-Poo, Mutt, or Stripes could even answer, Stick Dog spotted Karen himself. She was about halfway to them in the middle of the road and a good bit off to the left.

The Dizzy's Big GULP Coffee cup was back on her head. Stick Dog shot quick looks left and right down the street. He took some comfort in seeing there was no traffic at all.

"There she is," Stick Dog said to himself. He shook his head. "She can't see a thing. She's going to hurt herself."

The others saw what Stick Dog saw, but they didn't reach the same conclusion.

"It might not be her," Stripes said.

"You can't be sure," added Mutt.

Poo-Poo asked, "After all, Stick Dog, what are the odds the same exact dog would get her head stuck in the same exact cup two times in a row like that?"

"Apparently, with Karen, the odds are pretty good," whispered Stick Dog. It didn't sound like he was whispering to avoid detection by the man at the top of the pole. He remained turned away from them. It sounded more like Stick Dog was super-frustrated. He closed his eyes, counted to five, and then opened them again. Karen zigzagged back and forth across the single-dash line in the middle of the road. "I'm going to get her. Again."

"Don't eat her, Stick Dog!" Stripes said.

"Or drink her!" added Mutt.

"If it's even her, that is," said Poo-Poo.

When Stick Dog reached Karen, he did not lift her by the nape of the neck. Instead, he knocked the cup off her head, pointed to the truck where everybody else was, and nudged her in that direction.

Karen started running that way but stopped after just a couple of steps.

"Can I bring that cup, Stick Dog?"

He replied simply, "No."

They dashed to the side of the truck to join the others. The man at the top of the pole hadn't seen a thing. Poo-Poo, Mutt, and Stripes patted Karen on the back with great enthusiasm. They were happy to have their friend back.

"What were you doing?!" Stick Dog asked. "You could have been seen. Or hit by a car!"

Karen didn't seem to care at all. She answered matter-of-factly, "I wanted to make sure I got all the coffee out of that cup."

"Just stay here with us, okay?"

Karen nodded very fast. Then a question seemed to come immediately to her mind. She stopped nodding, started hopping up and down in place, looked directly at Stick Dog, and asked, "Can I run a few laps around the truck?! Can I, Stick Dog?"

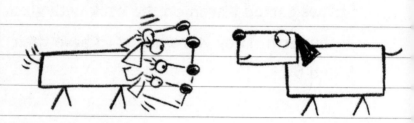

This was becoming too much—even for Stick Dog. He put his paws on Karen's shoulders to try to calm her down. He didn't push hard enough to hurt her—not even close. But he had to settle her body down a little.

"Look, Karen," he said as calmly as he could. "I need you to really focus on what I'm about to say to you. Pay really good attention, okay?"

"Is this about running laps around the truck, Stick Dog? Is it? Is it?!"

"No, it's not," Stick Dog said. He moved his paws from her shoulders to the sides of her face. He held her cheeks and stared straight into her eyes. "Listen, Karen. I think that coffee you drank has somehow affected you physically—and emotionally. You're talking really fast. And you're all jittery and stuff. That coffee made you super-hyper or something. And I'm afraid you might get hurt. I'm afraid you might run out in front of a car, or smash your head into something, or not be able to calm down when we're trying to hide from this human with the donuts. You HAVE to get hold of yourself."

Karen looked back into Stick Dog's eyes. She had listened closely.

"Okay, Stick Dog," she said. "I'll do my best. Totally. I will. For sure."

Stick Dog lowered his paws. "I know you will," he said to try to make her feel better. "Now, let's see if we can get some more of those donuts."

Stripes, Mutt, and Poo-Poo were obviously on board with this idea. They each drooled a little bit at the prospect of eating that sweet, doughy goodness.

"Good idea! Let's get all the donuts!" Karen said in agreement. "And when we do, maybe we'll find some more of that coffee too!"

Chapter 9

MUTT JIGGLES

It was a difficult choice for Stick Dog to make for his hungry friends.

There were ten donuts left in the box. Stick Dog had counted them when he snatched the pink one. But he knew it was highly likely the man would come down again soon. Stick Dog knew the man hadn't found his coffee cup up on the platform. Karen had taken the cup—and drunk all the coffee.

Stick Dog had a choice to make.

They could take all the donuts now, he thought.

If they did, the man would surely get mad—and suspicious—and keep a very close eye on his truck after that.

But Stick Dog suspected there might be more food in the truck or somewhere else close by. There was an idea nagging at the edge of Stick Dog's mind—but he just couldn't put his paw on it. His instincts told him there was more to accomplish here—he just hadn't figured it out yet.

The second option was to take just one more donut for now. The man might not notice, and they could get an additional opportunity to explore the truck—and the area. It would

provide Stick Dog a little more time to figure out what his instincts were trying to tell him.

He considered this choice when something happened.

And then something else happened.

A solitary breeze whooshed through the apple trees at the edge of the forest—and across the road. As the wind blew, it reached something in the center of the pavement.

Do you know what it was?

It was the coffee cup.

The empty Styrofoam coffee cup that Stick

Dog had knocked off Karen's head rolled
and bounced across the blacktop road. In
the silence of the still, cool morning, the
rattling cup made a lot of noise.

And that's when Stick Dog got his idea.

Do you know what it was?

Sorry. I can't tell you everything. I'll just
have to show you in the story.

Stick Dog risked peeking around the truck's
back bumper. He looked up at the top of
the pole. The man had heard the cup too

and looked down at the road from high up in the air. He put his hands on his hips, shook his head, and stepped from the platform back into the basket.

That's exactly what Stick Dog hoped would happen. He turned to Mutt, Poo-Poo, Stripes, and Karen.

The huge mechanical arm churned to life. The truck vibrated.

"We have to hide under the truck!" Stick Dog said urgently. He turned his head to watch the shadow of the giant metal arm in the grass. It came closer and closer. "I'll explain when we get under there. Go! Now!"

Stick Dog's seriousness was enough to

motivate the others. They dove under the
truck.

From beneath the truck they heard the arm
CLUNK! to a stop and its motor ease down
to silence. The truck stopped vibrating.
They heard the man step out of the basket.
They saw his work boots land on the
ground and begin to walk toward the road.
He got to the side of the road but had to
wait a minute as three cars passed.

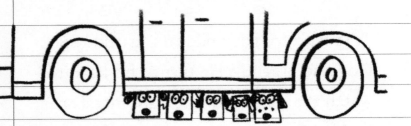

The dogs were arranged side by side under
the truck. Stick Dog was thankful that Mutt
was next to him.

"Mutt," he whispered. "Do you remember the spot in your fur where you stored that sharp nail? The nail we found earlier at Karen's favorite garbage can?"

"Of course, Stick Dog," answered Mutt, with absolute assurance. "I know where everything is. The nail is between the shoestring and a dented Ping-Pong ball I found last week. It's right behind my left shoulder blade."

"Can you shake the nail out for me?"

"I'd be happy to, Stick Dog."

With that, Mutt isolated the area behind his left shoulder blade and began to jiggle it. In just a few seconds, the nail fell out. Stick Dog picked it up with his mouth and dropped it right in front of himself.

After that, Stick Dog explained things very quickly.

"That man is going to pick up the coffee cup that Karen had on her head," Stick Dog whispered.

"He's going to be mighty disappointed," Karen interrupted proudly, and smiled. "I drank every last drop."

"I know you did," Stick Dog acknowledged,

and then continued. "This guy really wants some more coffee. I think he'll go get some more at that strange building down the road."

"That makes sense," Karen concurred, and nodded her head rapidly. She bumped it against the bottom of the truck a couple of times but didn't seem to notice. "Coffee is the most delicious, energizing, magical drink in the universe."

Stick Dog looked at Karen, who was still nodding (and bumping) her head. Then he continued to explain his strategy. "If he goes to get more coffee, as I suspect, then we'll have plenty of time to finish off those donuts and look for anything else around here."

Mutt cocked his head a little and looked at Stick Dog. He probably would have cocked his head a lot, but there wasn't much room underneath the truck.

"Stick Dog, it's a great plan and everything," he said. "But if he's going to retrieve more coffee, then he's going to take the truck— and the box of donuts—with him."

"Yeah, Stick Dog, what about that?" asked Poo-Poo.

"Leave it up to Stick Dog to forget the most important detail," Stripes said. She sounded almost proud that they had caught Stick Dog in a mistake. "Your plans never work out very well, Stick Dog. I'm sorry to say it, but it's true. If you would just listen, consider, and execute *our* food-snatching plans, things would really be a lot easier."

The other dogs nodded along with her comments.

"Like that time I wanted you to fly a helicopter for those frankfurters," Stripes said. "That could have worked."

"Or that time I wanted to steal the family car for those hamburgers," Poo-Poo said.

Stick Dog stared out at the worker as he listened. The traffic had passed, and the man was now in the middle of the road, holding the huge Styrofoam cup. He looked in it and turned it upside down and right side up in his hands. He appeared quite puzzled about why it was empty—and why it was out there in the middle of the road.

"He's not going to take the truck," Stick Dog said quietly to his comrades. "He's going to walk."

"He is?" asked Mutt. "But why?"

"Because his truck has a flat tire," Stick Dog answered quietly.

The others turned their heads in every direction to examine the truck's four tires. Poo-Poo spoke for them all when he said, "He doesn't have a flat tire, Stick Dog."

"No, he doesn't," said Stick Dog. And then he smiled. "Not yet."

Chapter 10

POP! H-OOO-SH!

Stick Dog watched the man stand in the middle of the road. He was confused. He looked into the empty cup again. Stick Dog was certain the man would return to the truck any second.

He turned to his friends and whispered, "Scooch out the other side. Run into the woods over there."

"But Stick Dog, there are apple trees on that side too," complained Poo-Poo. "I can't stand those things. The apples are SOOOO close, but we never get them."

Stick Dog listened as he watched the worker in the road. The man looked into the cup a final time. He shrugged, sighed, and pivoted. He was coming back.

"Don't worry about the apple trees," Stick Dog said quickly. "Hopefully, in a few minutes, we'll have a lot more donuts to eat."

Well, this was all Poo-Poo, Stripes, Karen, and Mutt needed to hear. They scooted backward on their bellies, emerged from beneath the truck on the other side, and sprinted to hide safely among the trees.

Stick Dog took the long, sharp nail and wedged it between one of the back tires and the ground. He pushed at it with his paw to ensure it was jammed in there nice and tight.

And then he raced to join his friends.

By the time Stick Dog dove into the woods to join them, the man was already back. He took his tool belt off and threw it into the truck. It clattered and clanged. He also took the donut box from the back bumper and slid it into the truck's bed.

"Need some more coffee," the man said to himself as he reached into his pocket to find his keys. "Don't even remember drinking my first cup."

"He's driving away! The donuts are leaving, Stick Dog!" Stripes exclaimed. "We'll never get them!"

"I knew this plan would never work," complained Poo-Poo.

"Oh no, Stick Dog! Oh no!" Karen said, and shook her head back and forth really fast.

Mutt pulled an old shoestring from his fur

and began to chew on it nervously.

"Wait for it," Stick Dog whispered. "Wait for it."

The worker continued to talk to himself as he climbed into the truck. "Need to finish this job, then get to the guys at the next job," he said. "I told them I'd bring the donuts this morning. But first, coffee. Dizzy's has the best."

"Wait for it," Stick Dog whispered again.

The truck began to roll forward. It moved only a few inches before the dogs heard two distinct sounds.

POP! H-OOO-SH!

The back left tire deflated instantly.

Karen, Poo-Poo, Mutt, and Stripes yelped with glee.

"The donuts are staying, Stick Dog!" Stripes exclaimed. "We're going to get them!"

"I knew this plan would work," said Poo-Poo.

"Oh yes, Stick Dog! Oh yes!" Karen said, and nodded her head up and down really fast.

Mutt pushed the old shoestring back into his fur.

"Okay. Everybody settle down," Stick Dog said, and smiled. He knew only the first part of his plan was accomplished. He watched as the man—who had obviously heard the *POP! H-OOO-SH!* sounds through his open window—turned off the engine and climbed back out of the truck.

The worker stood there with his back to Stick Dog and his pals. He stared at the flat tire. His hands were on his hips. His shoulders slumped forward. He tapped his right work boot against the ground seven times.

The man looked down the street toward the donut shop. The giant donut and coffee cup spun slowly around, reflecting and flashing the sun's brightness with each revolution. They were like beacons in the sky. The

worker looked up and felt the sun's warmth
against his face.

And then he said exactly what Stick Dog
hoped to hear.

"I'll fix this later," the man said, and smiled
a little bit. He tossed his hard hat into the
crane's basket. "It's such a nice day. I think
I'll walk."

He reached into the donut box in the back of the truck, seemed puzzled briefly, but then took one out. This donut was covered in dark brown goo. He took a huge bite and then started walking down the road.

"He took another one of our donuts!" exclaimed Poo-Poo, clearly aghast.

"The nerve!" exclaimed Stripes.

"Thief!" Karen yelled. Then she began

chasing her tail again.

Mutt scratched himself behind his ear.

"There are plenty more," Stick Dog said, and watched as the man walked farther and farther away from the truck—and closer and closer to Dizzy's Donuts. After a few minutes, when the man was almost halfway there, Stick Dog announced, "It's donut time."

The dogs hurtled out of the forest and raced toward the truck.

Karen was in the lead.

Chapter 11

DONUTS AND AN IDEA

When he reached the truck, Stick Dog
promptly propped himself up on the
truck's rear bumper. He grasped the donut
box from the back of the truck with his
mouth and brought it down to the ground.
He flipped the flaps, peered inside, and
counted.

"There are nine more donuts in here," Stick Dog said. "That works out perfectly. You all get two each."

To their good fortune, there was a wide variety of flavors. Two were sprinkled with white powder, two were covered in a dark brown substance, and two had a shiny glaze to them. There were two more pink ones with speckles. Finally, there was one that had no hole and looked like a deflated ball. It looked exactly like the first one Stick Dog saw the worker eat earlier—the one with the red, liquidy center. Poo-Poo got that one.

It made no difference to any of them which
donuts they received—they were all sweet
and delicious. Stick Dog passed out two
to each of his friends and then took the
remaining donut—a glazed one—for himself.

They devoured their first donuts quickly.
They bit and chewed and swallowed—
and smiled—the whole time. When they
started in on their second donuts, however,
Poo-Poo suddenly stopped eating.

Something was wrong.

Very wrong.

"S-Stick D-D-Dog?" Poo-Poo asked. It was clear just from his voice that something troubled him greatly.

"Yes?" answered Stick Dog as he stepped closer. He had finished his one donut and was now simply watching the others enjoy their second courses. "What is it, Poo-Poo?"

"M-M-My d-donut."

"What about it?"

"I th-think I k-killed it."

This was such a startling statement that Stripes, Mutt, and Karen stopped eating and raised their heads to see what was happening.

"What do you mean?" asked Stick Dog.

"Look at it," Poo-Poo said, and pointed to his donut on the ground. "It's bleeding."

This comment brought Karen, Mutt, and Stripes closer to examine the donut. Stick Dog was about to explain the red liquid center to Poo-Poo, but he decided to wait just a moment before doing so. He wanted to listen to the others for a few seconds.

"It's bleeding, all right," Stripes said, and looked at the dripping red liquid emerging from the donut's center.

Karen shook her head and said, "You really shouldn't hurt the things you love, Poo-Poo."

Mutt nodded in agreement. He said, "That really is pretty rude, Poo-Poo."

Poo-Poo turned to Stick Dog. "I didn't mean to hurt it. I really didn't."

Stick Dog came closer and looked Poo-Poo directly in the eyes. "You didn't hurt it," he said, trying hard to suppress a grin. "You can't hurt something that was never alive."

"Excuse me, Stick Dog," Poo-Poo said. "But if something bleeds from inside, it's alive."

"Why don't you taste that red liquidy stuff?" Stick Dog suggested. "You'll see."

"That's disgusting! Are you crazy?!" screamed Poo-Poo immediately. "I'm not a, umm, umm . . . leprechaun!"

Mutt, Karen, and Stripes looked equally aghast at Stick Dog's idea.

"I think you mean 'vampire,'" said Stick Dog calmly. He then stepped even closer and held his right paw above the red liquid. "May I?"

"Go ahead," Poo-Poo said. "Yuck!"

Stick Dog dipped the tip of his paw into the center of the donut. He withdrew it, eyed the thick red drip on his paw—and then licked it off. It tasted like sugary strawberries. The taste perfectly matched the scent he had smelled earlier.

It was totally delicious.

And it showed on Stick Dog's expression.

Well, this instantly changed Poo-Poo's entire attitude and demeanor. He stepped forward and dipped his own paw into the red liquid. He brought it to his mouth, hesitated a single second, and then licked it off.

"No way," Poo-Poo said. He turned to Karen, Mutt, and Stripes. "You guys are not going to believe this."

"What?" asked Stripes.

"That donut's blood tastes like strawberries."

"It's not blood," Stick Dog said. "It's like

smashed up, liquefied strawberries. It was
never alive."

Poo-Poo looked doubtfully at Stick Dog.
Then he looked down to the ground where
the rest of the donut waited for him. He
could still taste the sweet strawberry flavor
in his mouth.

And then his face softened.

Suddenly, Poo-Poo didn't even seem to care
anymore. He leaned down to the donut.
His mouth hovered just one inch above it.

"Whatever," he whispered, and shrugged.
He picked the donut up in his mouth and
finished it in three
bites.

Mutt, Stripes, and Karen returned to finishing their second donuts as well.

Stick Dog was happy to have the "bleeding donut" crisis behind them so quickly. His only concern now was if the worker was coming back. Every minute or so, he glanced down the road to make certain the man was not returning. He knew that once he saw the man, they would have to leave.

But for now the man was nowhere in sight, his friends happily munched away at their donuts, and the sun was bright and warm overhead. Stick Dog leaned back against the truck, lifted his head to the sun, and closed his eyes—purely happy and satisfied that their donut mission had succeeded. It felt so nice for Stick Dog to rest there in the sun's warmth.

In twelve seconds, Poo-Poo said, "I'm still hungry."

Quickly, Mutt, Karen, and Stripes expressed the same sentiment. Stick Dog grinned a bit to himself and opened his eyes. For a split second, he was blinded by the sunshine. He blinked three times. Dots of white light danced in his vision as his eyes acclimated to the brightness. When the white dots faded, they were replaced with different dots.

Red dots.

The dots slowly took shape.

Apples.

And Stick Dog figured out what his instincts had been telling him.

Stick Dog had an idea.

He stood up, stretched his legs, and cast a knowing eye at those apples. There were dozens of them in every tree. Stick Dog knew that if he could fill the donut box with apples, then they'd all have plenty to eat today—and maybe even have some apples left over for tomorrow.

They had all tasted one of those apples before—about this time in late summer last year. They had romped through the woods searching for wild blackberry bushes when they came across this tiny, abandoned orchard with the road passing through it.

That day a strong random wind whooshed through the forest just as they went through the orchard. The wind shook a single apple off its stem. It fell to the ground, and the dogs formed a circle and each dog took a bite and rolled it to the next one.

Stick Dog remembered that flavor—tart and sweet. He remembered the crunch when his teeth broke through the shiny red-and-yellow skin. He remembered the juice as it dripped down his chin.

It was the only apple any of them had ever tasted.

And now he was going to get them some more.

Mutt, Karen, Stripes, and Poo-Poo stared at Stick Dog. He smiled and seemed lost in his own thoughts. His friends had never seen him like this. He was always alert, continually aware of his surroundings, and constantly looking out for his friends. But now, just for this moment, it looked like he was daydreaming.

Karen asked the question the others were all thinking. "Stick Dog, what's going on with you?"

Stick Dog said, "I was just remembering that day we tasted an apple."

"Don't remind us!" Stripes said instantly.

"Yeah, Stick Dog," Poo-Poo added. "That's torture."

Mutt looked up into the trees, frowned, and shook his head in sincere and genuine disappointment.

Karen started chasing her tail again.

"It's only torture," Stick Dog said, and
lowered his gaze to look at his companions.
"If we can't get them."

"We CAN'T!" Stripes declared loudly.
"That's the TORTURE part!"

With that, Stick Dog took a few steps
toward the truck—and toward the basket at
the end of the crane.

Stick Dog glanced down the road in both directions—and saw nothing.

He climbed into the basket at the end of the long, mechanical arm. He stepped around the hard hat on the basket floor. Stick Dog stood on his hind legs and propped his front legs up on the control box. It was easy for him to lean forward and balance this way.

Stick Dog looked down at the joystick and buttons on the control panel. There was one green button off to the right that was bigger than the others.

He pressed it.

And the motor inside the crane whirred and vibrated to life.

Chapter 12

THE RISE OF STICK DOG

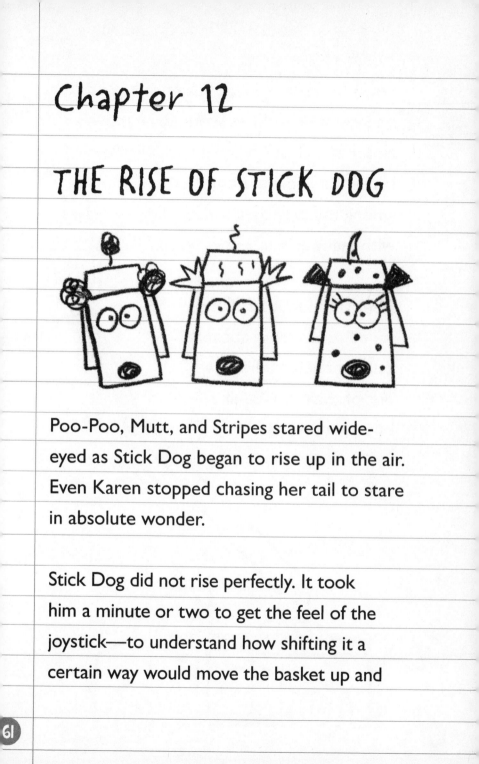

Poo-Poo, Mutt, and Stripes stared wide-eyed as Stick Dog began to rise up in the air. Even Karen stopped chasing her tail to stare in absolute wonder.

Stick Dog did not rise perfectly. It took him a minute or two to get the feel of the joystick—to understand how shifting it a certain way would move the basket up and

down or left and right. But once he had
a sense of how things worked, he moved
closer and closer toward an apple tree.
In no time, he was immersed
among the branches and leaves
with many apples within reach.

"Get the donut box!" he
yelled down from above.
This startled his friends
out of their trance-like
observations.

"There aren't any donuts left in there!" Poo-Poo yelled up. "We ate them all. Remember? And since you're up there with all those apples, don't you think you should pick some for us to eat? I mean, I don't think donuts are just going to magically appear in the box again. You know what I mean?"

Karen whispered, "Stick Dog rarely knows what he's doing." Then she decided that running laps around the truck as fast as she could was the best thing to do at the moment. And that's what she did.

Stick Dog eyed the street in both directions before responding to the others. The good news was, the worker was not walking back from the donut shop yet. The bad news was that a car—a bright-yellow convertible—approached from the opposite direction. It was still very far off, but Stick Dog knew cars could move fast. He didn't have much time. "We'll use the empty box to bring the apples back to my pipe. We can fit a bunch in there."

"Oh, good idea! I was just about to think of that!" Poo-Poo called. He opened the flaps, preparing the box to hold as many apples as possible.

Poo-Poo, Mutt, and Stripes gathered beneath Stick Dog.

Karen started her fourth lap around
the truck.

And Stick Dog
began to drop
apples down.

Only a few of the apples were actually
caught. Most plopped onto the soft green
grass, bounced a couple of times, and rolled
to a gentle stop. One hit Poo-Poo right on
top of his head. He smiled after the impact.

From then on, Poo-Poo
began to dart this way and
that way, trying to get hit
again.

He succeeded twice.

It was a speedy process. By the time Karen had finished her seventh lap around the truck, Stick Dog had dropped more than a dozen apples to Mutt, Poo-Poo, and Stripes. He glanced down to see that the donut box was full of apples. He stopped picking and dropping them, and snapped his head left to look down the road toward the donut shop. The worker was, thankfully, still nowhere in sight. When he turned his head in the other direction, however, the news was not nearly as positive.

The yellow convertible was much closer than Stick Dog anticipated. It was traveling at a high rate of speed—and would be to the truck in seconds.

Stick Dog yelled only one word.

And he yelled it fast.

"Hide!"

That was all his friends needed to hear. Poo-Poo, Mutt, and Stripes dove back under the truck. Karen raced one more lap around it and miraculously noticed that the others were all missing. She stopped, heard them call from beneath the truck, and dove under too.

Stick Dog saw that his friends were safe.

And he saw something else too.

The yellow convertible was much closer, had four human passengers—and was slowing down. Stick Dog had seen this kind of behavior before on Highway 16 on top of the hill above his pipe. Traffic slowed down when work trucks were on the side of the road.

But Stick Dog didn't want this car to slow down now. He only had a few seconds until it was close enough for the driver and passengers to see him. Stick Dog couldn't maneuver the arm down—that would take way too long. He couldn't crouch very low—the basket was too narrow.

Stick Dog had only one idea.

He snatched the hard hat from the basket floor and pulled it onto his head, yanking it down as far as he could.

Rather than turn suddenly away from the yellow convertible, Stick Dog looked straight down as it slowly passed beneath the long, jointed mechanical arm. The front-seat passenger, a woman, stared into the rearview mirror and applied lipstick. The driver, a man, talked on his phone and didn't look up at all. He was far too wrapped up in his conversation—gesticulating with his arms and hands as he spoke—to notice something like a dog in a hard hat at the top of a mechanical crane.

But the two passengers in the backseat, a girl and a boy, were smart, curious, and inquisitive. They saw a crane and wanted to know why it was there and what kind of work was being done.

And who was doing it.

So they looked at the person in the basket.

And saw that it wasn't a person at all.

It was a dog.

It was Stick Dog.

They saw him, and their eyes flashed open in shock and surprise.

And then they passed under the crane.

Stick Dog didn't know, of course, what happened in the car next. He watched to make sure it didn't stop, turn around, and return to see a dog at the end of a crane in an apple tree.

It didn't. It just kept driving down the road past the donut shop—and out of sight.

Stick Dog suspected the little humans told the big humans what they had seen. He also suspected the big humans didn't believe them and continued to put on their makeup and talk on the phone.

"All clear!" Stick Dog yelled, and took off the hard hat. "You can come out now!"

Mutt, Karen, Poo-Poo, and Stripes emerged from beneath the truck.

"One more apple drop and then we better get out of here!" Stick Dog called. He manipulated the joystick and directed the basket down to the lowest branch of the tree. He saw a big red apple there. It looked perfectly delectable. This would be the last one.

His friends gathered under Stick Dog, waiting for the bright-red fruit to fall. Poo-Poo hoped he could get one more, just one more, knock on the head.

Stick Dog steered the basket exactly where he wanted. He reached for the last apple.

But he didn't pick it.

Do you know why?

I'll tell you.

Farther down the branch, closer to the trunk, something caught his eye.

Something moved.

Something twitched.

It was gray.

It was puffy.

Stick Dog slowly maneuvered the crane back out of the tree and away from this lowest branch. He looked down at his friends on the ground.

"Poo-Poo!" Stick Dog called quietly. "Stay right there! I'm coming to get you!"

While Stick Dog descended, Mutt, Karen, Stripes, and Poo-Poo waited next to the truck. They were extremely curious about why Stick Dog suddenly wanted to come get Poo-Poo.

"He probably needs my help," Poo-Poo suggested to the others as Stick Dog descended. "I mean, let's face it. I really am the alpha dog here. It's no surprise that Stick Dog needs me to finish the job. Frankly, I'm surprised he didn't summon me earlier."

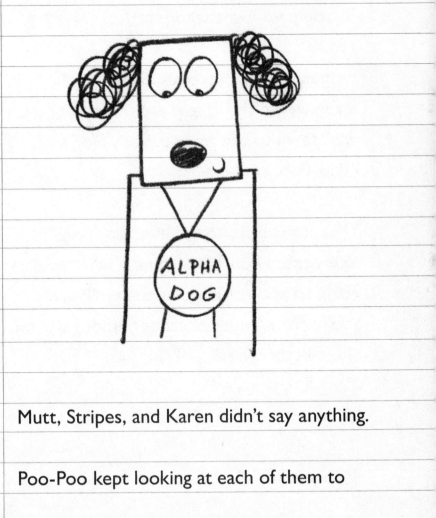

Mutt, Stripes, and Karen didn't say anything.

Poo-Poo kept looking at each of them to

gain verification of his alpha-dog-ness. An awkward silence hung in the air among them.

But only for eight seconds.

Because in eight seconds, Stick Dog had maneuvered the long crane the rest of the way down to the ground. Stick Dog said, "Poo-Poo, you're—"

"You don't need to tell me, Stick Dog," interrupted Poo-Poo. "I know what you're going to say. You're going to say, 'Poo-Poo, you're the obvious alpha dog among us. You should take over.'"

"Umm, no, I wasn't," said Stick Dog.

"Are you sure?"

"Pretty sure," Stick Dog answered. "I was going to say, you're—"

"A brave and noble alpha dog?" Poo-Poo said, attempting to finish Stick Dog's sentence again.

"Umm, no," Stick Dog repeated. "You're—"

"Brilliant, fierce, and loyal?" Poo-Poo tried again.

"No. You're—"

"Really handsome and charming?"

"No. You're—"

"Alpha-tastic?"

Stick Dog waited a few seconds. Then he asked, "Can I finish my sentence, please?"

"Sure, go ahead," Poo-Poo answered. He seemed slightly relieved that he could quit guessing. "As alpha, I give you permission."

"Thanks. I appreciate that," Stick Dog said. "Here's what I was going to say: You're about to get the chance you've always wanted. There's a squirrel up there."

Poo-Poo instantly crouched down and SPRANG up, soaring through the air toward the mechanical arm's basket. He landed right outside its door, lunged in so quickly that he

bonked his head against its wall, didn't care—
and stretched up on his hind legs right at Stick
Dog's side. He whipped his head around to
stare at Stick Dog.

There was controlled fury and complete
determination chiseled into his expression.

His jaw was firmly set. His eyes were squinted. He whispered, "Let's go!"

Stick Dog placed his paws on the joystick and began their ascent toward the apple tree's lowest branch—and the squirrel who was up there.

Chapter 13

DOG VS. SQUIRREL

On the short trip up, Poo-Poo peppered
Stick Dog with rapid-fire questions.

"Are you sure it's a squirrel?"

"I'm sure," Stick Dog answered as he
steered the basket back up into the tree. He
also shot looks in both directions down the
street. No humans were in sight.

"Did it have a puffy tail? Squirrels have puffy
tails."

"It did."

"Was it gray? Squirrels around here are
gray."

"It's gray."

"Whiskers? Twitching whiskers? How about
those?! Did it have those? Did it?! Huh!?"

"I couldn't tell," answered Stick Dog. "I only
saw the tail."

"You sure it was a squirrel? Not a raccoon?
Or a bird? Or a cow?"

Stick Dog took his paws off the joystick.
The basket stopped climbing. He looked at
Poo-Poo. "A cow? In a tree?"

"It's possible," Poo-Poo answered slowly as he considered this option. Then three seconds later he remembered where they were and what they were doing. "I'm just so excited! I've waited so long for this chance! It's like a beautiful dream finally coming true. I'm not dreaming, am I, Stick Dog? Please tell me I'm not."

"You're not," Stick Dog said. He moved the joystick again to continue the basket's rise.

"I know how to make sure," Poo-Poo whispered to himself. He then banged his forehead twice into the side of the basket. He rubbed his head and looked at Stick Dog with a smile. "It's not a dream! That hurt! That REALLY hurt!!"

"I'm glad," Stick Dog answered, and shook his head a little. He manipulated the basket to the lowest branch.

"Please still be here. Please be here," Poo-Poo whispered as he squeezed his eyes shut and clasped his paws. "Plee-eee-ease!"

Stick Dog eased the basket a little farther into the tree and took his paws off the joystick. The motor sighed to a stop. The crane stopped moving. And Stick Dog peered toward the tree trunk. On the opposite side, he saw the puffy tail sticking out. The squirrel was still there.

"Is he there?" Poo-Poo whispered. His eyes were still closed. "Please, oh please, tell me he is."

"He's still there," Stick Dog whispered back. "I can see his tail."

"Is it twitching?"

"It is," whispered Stick Dog.

"Erggh! I can't stand it when they do that!"

growled Poo-Poo as quietly as he could. "Where is he?"

"There. Behind the trunk," responded Stick Dog. "You can only see his tail."

Stick Dog had parked the basket right next to the wide, thick branch. Fortunately, it was kind of flat on top. He was fairly confident that Poo-Poo could keep his balance on it. And since it was the lowest branch, Stick Dog felt that Poo-Poo would be okay even if he did fall.

"I think you can go now," Stick Dog said. "Be careful. And be as quiet as you can."

Poo-Poo narrowed his eyes. "I'm going in."

He pushed his left shoulder against the
basket door. He took his first step onto the
branch, his paw pads easing quietly down
onto the tree bark.

Poo-Poo was halfway out of the basket
when he took his second step.

But it wasn't as quiet as the first.

He stepped on a small twig jutting out of the wide, flat branch.

In a third of a second, the squirrel's head peeked out from the other side of the tree trunk.

Now, you would think a squirrel who had just noticed two dogs up in the tree might scurry along or jump to another branch— or begin shaking or chattering.

It did none of these things.

It didn't move at all. It stared at Poo-Poo with cold, fierce eyes.

"You're not afraid, huh?" Poo-Poo whispered with both surprise and defiance in his voice. He spoke quietly through clenched teeth. "Well, neither am I. I'm coming after you! I've been waiting my whole life for this one-and-only chance!"

Stick Dog listened—he had never heard such pure rage and determination from Poo-Poo before. He watched in silence—transfixed by the confrontation.

Poo-Poo was fully out of the basket now. He wriggled his paws on the branch a bit to ensure absolute footing and balance. He lowered his head—ready to charge. He couldn't even see the squirrel in this position. It didn't matter. Everything about Poo-Poo—his anger, his conviction, his sense of justice and superiority—had driven him to this one moment in his life. This one moment in time.

When he lowered his head, the squirrel emerged completely from behind the trunk.

"Time to meet your density, Mr. Squirrel!" Poo-Poo growled. He lowered his head even farther and leaned back on his rear haunches. He got ready to lunge and bash.

"Wait!"

It was Stick Dog.

Poo-Poo shifted his weight forward and steadied himself again. He didn't lift his head. His body trembled in anticipation. He whispered, "Why?"

"It's not a 'mister' squirrel," Stick Dog answered quickly. "It's a 'missus' squirrel."

"Who cares?" Poo-Poo hissed.

"And she has a baby."

Poo-Poo lifted his head out of its battering-ram position. He looked at the squirrel with narrowed, menacing eyes. And he saw the baby squirrel in her arms.

Poo-Poo's eyes widened—and his expression softened.

The baby squirrel was so small.

So small.

The mother squirrel held it so close.

So close.

But squirrels were Poo-Poo's archenemies.

Archenemies.

This might be his only chance to get one.

Only chance.

"Poo-Poo?" Stick Dog whispered.

He didn't answer. He stood motionless.

"Poo-Poo?"

"Stick Dog," Poo-Poo whispered back. He
waited a few seconds and blinked his eyes
several times. His body stopped trembling.
"It's the tiniest, most beautiful thing I've
ever seen."

Stick Dog smiled.

And Poo-Poo took another step—
backward into the basket.

Chapter 14

TELLING THE TRUTH

While Poo-Poo stared blankly out from the basket, Stick Dog backed it out of the tree. He paused just a moment to pick that final big, red, delectable apple. He dropped it down to Mutt, Karen, and Stripes. When he dropped it, the basket shook a bit, bumped the branch, and knocked a second apple loose.

Stripes saw the two apples fall in succession. "Hey!" she said. "Two for one special!"

Stick Dog hesitated. Something at the edge of his mind bothered him again. Another instinct.

He whispered to himself, "Two for one special. Two for one special."

Then he snapped his head down and peered into the back of the truck. He *knew* there was something else there. He just *knew* it.

The worker said he would bring donuts for the men at his next job. What did the sticker say on that first box? Stick Dog tried to remember.

And then he *did* remember.

And he saw what he sought immediately. He could just see the corner of it poking out from beneath the worker's jacket—the one that had fluttered down into the back of the truck like a parachute.

He didn't say a word. He looked at Poo-Poo, who stared blankly into the tree's branches. Stick Dog put his paw on the joystick and continued their descent toward the others.

It was a short, slow, and quiet ride down to the ground in the basket. Poo-Poo said nothing. There was a mixture of disappointment and wonder on his face—as if he didn't quite know how to feel. His eyelids drooped with discouragement, but there was a trace of a smile on his face.

When Stick Dog and Poo-Poo stepped out of the basket, their friends were ready with questions.

"What happened up there?" Stripes wanted to know.

"Did Poo-Poo get the squirrel?" inquired Mutt.

"Did you find any coffee?!" asked Karen. She then plopped down on her belly and barely lifted her chin off the ground to speak. "All of a sudden, I feel really tired. I think some more coffee might help."

Stick Dog turned to Poo-Poo. He wanted to give him the opportunity to answer all these inquiries himself.

"There was no coffee," Poo-Poo said, and lifted his head. "And there *was* a squirrel. Two squirrels, in fact."

This answer sparked his friends' curiosity even more. Stripes asked the question that was on all their minds. "Did you prove your superiority to them?"

Poo-Poo began to speak, but no words came out.

And Stick Dog stepped forward, closer to Stripes, Mutt, and Karen—and closer to the donut box that was now absolutely full of red apples.

"Did Poo-Poo prove his superiority to squirrels?" Stick Dog said, repeating the question. "He did. He most definitely did."

Mutt and Stripes began to hop and yelp and swish their tails madly. Karen, reenergized by this momentous news, pushed herself up off the ground and hopped up and down too. They gathered around Poo-Poo. They congratulated him. They patted him on the back.

Stick Dog waited for them to calm down. Once, for the briefest moment, during all the back slaps and yelping, Stick Dog caught Poo-Poo's eye. And Poo-Poo smiled at him.

"It's time to go!" Stick Dog yelled. He looked down the road to the right. No cars were coming. He looked down the road to the left. No cars were coming.

But the worker was. He was about halfway back—and he held another giant cup of coffee.

The others saw him too.

"Stick Dog?!" Karen asked. "Can we stay and try to get his coffee again? PLEASE?!"

"No," Stick Dog answered simply and definitively. He double-checked the road to ensure there was no traffic. "But when we get back to my pipe, you can bite into some of these apples and drink all the juice."

Karen smiled. Then she raced across the street and into the woods in the general direction of Stick Dog's pipe.

Mutt and Stripes followed immediately after her.

"Stick Dog?" Poo-Poo asked.

"Yes?"

"Thanks."

"Hey," Stick Dog said, and used his front left paw to close the lid on the donut box the best he could. It was really full. He continued, "All I did was tell the truth."

"Really?"

"Of course," Stick Dog explained. "You had a choice to make. By choosing not to prove your superiority to squirrels, you actually proved your superiority to squirrels."

"Huh?"

"You showed restraint. You showed absolute

control. You could have taught that squirrel a lesson," Stick Dog said. "But you didn't need to. You didn't have to prove anything—to the squirrel, to me, to yourself. You know who you are."

Poo-Poo scrunched up his face as he contemplated Stick Dog's words. He tilted his head skyward. Then he began to smile just a little bit. "I'm Poo-Poo."

"That's right. You're Poo-Poo."

Poo-Poo lowered his head and looked right

into Stick Dog's eyes. "Stick Dog," he said.
"You're not going to believe this."

"Believe what?"

"I actually understand what you mean."

"That doesn't surprise me a bit," Stick Dog
said, and triple-checked for traffic. He
pushed the box of apples toward Poo-Poo.
"Can you carry these back to my pipe?
I have one more thing I need to do here."

"I'd be happy to," Poo-Poo said, and nodded.
He picked the box up with his mouth. His
first couple of steps were awkward, but once
he understood the weight of the box and
how it swung, it was pretty easy. Poo-Poo
crossed the street and entered the woods
to track down Stripes, Karen, and Mutt, and

continue the journey to Stick Dog's pipe.

Once Stick Dog saw that Poo-Poo was into the woods safely, he hurried to the back of the truck.

The worker was only a few hundred feet away now.

Quickly, Stick Dog propped himself up on the truck's bumper. He yanked at the sleeve of the man's jacket in the back of the truck. He pulled it all the way out and allowed it to fall to the ground.

And the thing Stick Dog sought revealed itself fully.

Stick Dog pulled it closer.

He looked at the sticker on the box.

"Two for one special!" Stick Dog read and smiled. "Buy one box, get another free!"

Stick Dog flipped the flaps of this second donut box. There were thirteen sweet, colorful, scrumptious donuts inside.

He closed the lid. He clenched the box in his mouth and dropped to all fours. He scampered to the street and saw that the worker was still a good distance away. He had his Big GULP Coffee cup tilted up in front of his face as he drank and walked.

He never saw Stick Dog.

Stick Dog checked for traffic. He couldn't wait to share a second box of Dizzy's Donuts with Mutt, Karen, Stripes, and Poo-Poo. They would be so surprised.

As Stick Dog hurried across the road, the pavement felt smooth and warm beneath his paws.

THE END

Move over Stick Dog;
there's a new pet in town!

Read on for a sneak peek of
Tom Watson's new series STICK CAT!
Coming soon!

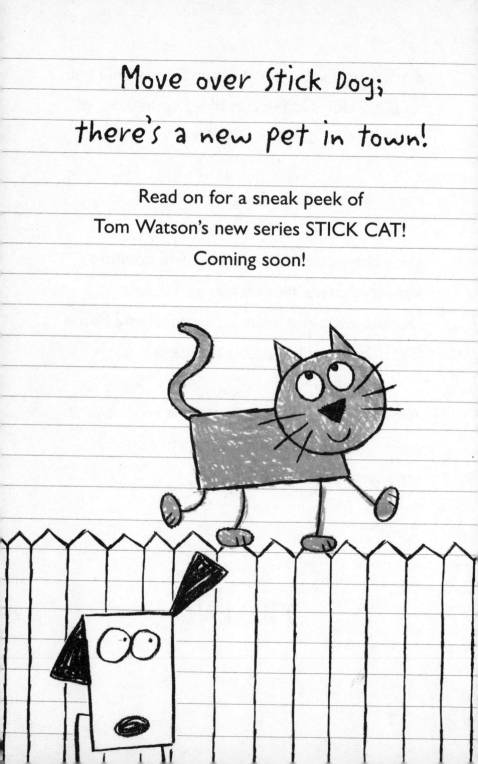

Chapter 1

REMEMBER OUR DEAL?

Do you remember our deal from the Stick Dog books? You know, how you're *not* allowed to hassle me about my drawing skills and stuff? And how I *am* allowed to go off in other directions now and then?

I'm glad you remember, because I have a bit of a situation here. I need to go off in a *way* different direction.

A NEW DEAL

YOU   TW ME

And it's Mary's fault.

Who's Mary? Good question.

Let me just tell you how this all got started.

Mary Cunningham
walked by my desk
on the way to the
pencil sharpener
yesterday.

MARY

She paused for a
second at my desk
and said, "Hi."

It was weird. She had never said hi to me
before.

It was right in the middle of Ms. Griffin's

English class. I was about to get cranking on a new Stick Dog story. It is pretty much my favorite part of every school day.

Mary sharpened her pencil and returned to her seat. One minute later the super-weird stuff began.

Mary came back.

This was her second trip to the pencil sharpener. Only this time she didn't just pause at my desk—she stopped. I know you probably think I'm making this up, but I'm not. I swear. She actually stopped.

Mary tapped her pencil on my composition book as she stood there right next to me. Her pencil has a little rubber cat eraser on it. It jiggled with each tap.

She has cat everything. Her folders and book covers have cats on them. She has cat sweaters and pencils and socks. I've noticed her talking a lot about her cats, Francis and Nora.

Can I tell you something weird? I don't know how it happened or when it happened, but something occurred last week or last month or whenever, and now girls are a lot less annoying and a lot more, you know, interesting.

And Mary is more interesting than any other girl in my class.

She stopped tapping her pencil and looked at me. The little orange-and-white cat eraser wobbled an extra couple of seconds after the pencil stopped moving. Mary stood real close on the left side of my desk.

It started to get warm in class for some reason.

I wondered if maybe Ms. Griffin should open a window.

"Are you working on another Stick Dog story?" Mary asked.

I nodded.

"What kind of food will they discover this time?"

"I'm thinking about candy," I answered. "A Halloween story maybe."

"That's a fun idea."

Okay, this was more than a walking-by-my-desk-on-the-way-to-the-pencil-sharpener comment. This was an official conversation.

I said, "I think it could be really funny if they follow two kids around the neighborhood on Halloween. And maybe they get all freaked out by the costumes and stuff."

That's when Mary did this really cool thing.

She laughed.

"You should do a story about cats," she suggested. "I have cats."

"Yeah, maybe." I didn't know what else to say.

6

"I'd like to read it if you do."

Then she left.

I only said one thing after Mary sat down at her desk again.

"Ms. Griffin," I called. "Can I open a window? It's really warm in here."

Chapter 2

STICK CAT AND GOOSE

Okay, this feline creature is going to need a name. I've thought about it for a very, very long time. And I've considered my own drawing abilities. I've chosen a name.

This is Stick Cat.

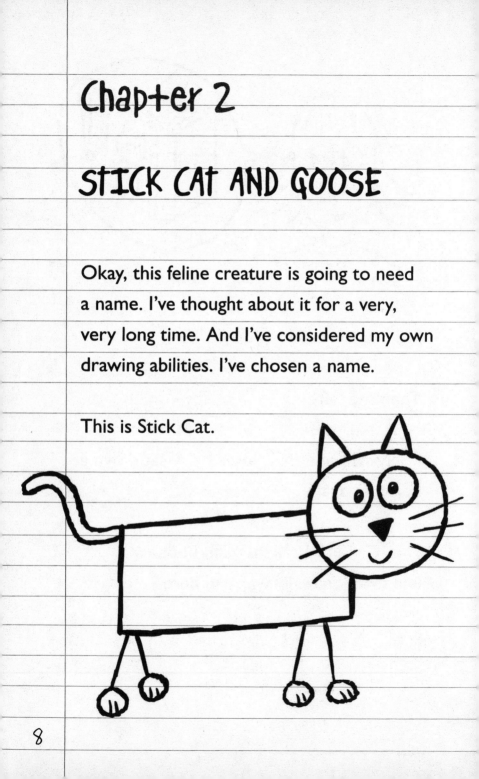

Stick Cat lives in an apartment on the twenty-third floor of a big building in the city. It's kind of an old building. Stick Cat has a human roommate named Goose. I know, I know. Goose is a very strange name for a human. But this is the only thing Stick Cat has ever heard his roommate called. So that's that.

STICK CAT'S APARTMENT

Between you and me, this guy has a neck that looks a little out of proportion with his head and the rest of his body. And my guess is that somewhere back in grade school—

when it's really important to call people by anything *except* their real names—someone commented on his long neck, nicknamed him Goose, and now he's stuck with it.

That's just a guess. I don't know for sure.

Goose is not embarrassed by his name at all. In fact, he's embraced it. There are geese all around the apartment. He has goose pillows on the couch. He has a picture of geese flying above a field hung over the mantel in the living room. There is a neon sign in the kitchen that says "Goose Island Root Beer." It's really colorful, with lots of orange and green tubular lights. Stick Cat likes it during the day but can't stand how much it glows at night if Goose forgets to turn it off.

Goose works in the city. Every morning during the week, Stick Cat watches Goose eat his breakfast and brush his teeth. Then Goose checks his pockets for his wallet, keys, and phone, and walks over to where Stick Cat is sitting on the windowsill. This is Stick Cat's favorite place.

It's where he can see another old building across the alley. That building is a lot like Stick Cat's, but instead of apartments, it has mainly businesses—an old piano factory is on a bunch of the upper floors. At street level, there is a piano store and a bakery. From this sill, he can also see the pigeons. There are dozens of pigeons that live in the alley and fly back and forth and perch on the window ledges of both buildings.

Anyway, this is where Stick Cat likes to sit the most—and it's where Goose comes every morning to do three things.

He opens the window a couple of inches so Stick Cat can feel a little breeze in his favorite spot.

Goose pats Stick Cat on the head.